KRAKEN ME UP

FAIR

KRAKEN ME UP

JEFFREY EBBELER

HOLIDAY HOUSE • NEW YORK

Bring in your pets.
My dog is purebred.
My cat has won first five times.

My horse is fast.
My lizard is the best.
My mouse will win.
I hope they like us.

Pretty pig.

A fine hen.
I love this llama.

It is a . . .

It is a . . .

Kraken!

Krakens are
big.
Krakens are
scary.
Krakens are
mean.
The kraken will
eat us.

A kraken can eat a ship!

He is not scary.
He is not mean.
He is . . .
. . . shy.

I met him at my home by the sea.

I was alone.
I was sad.

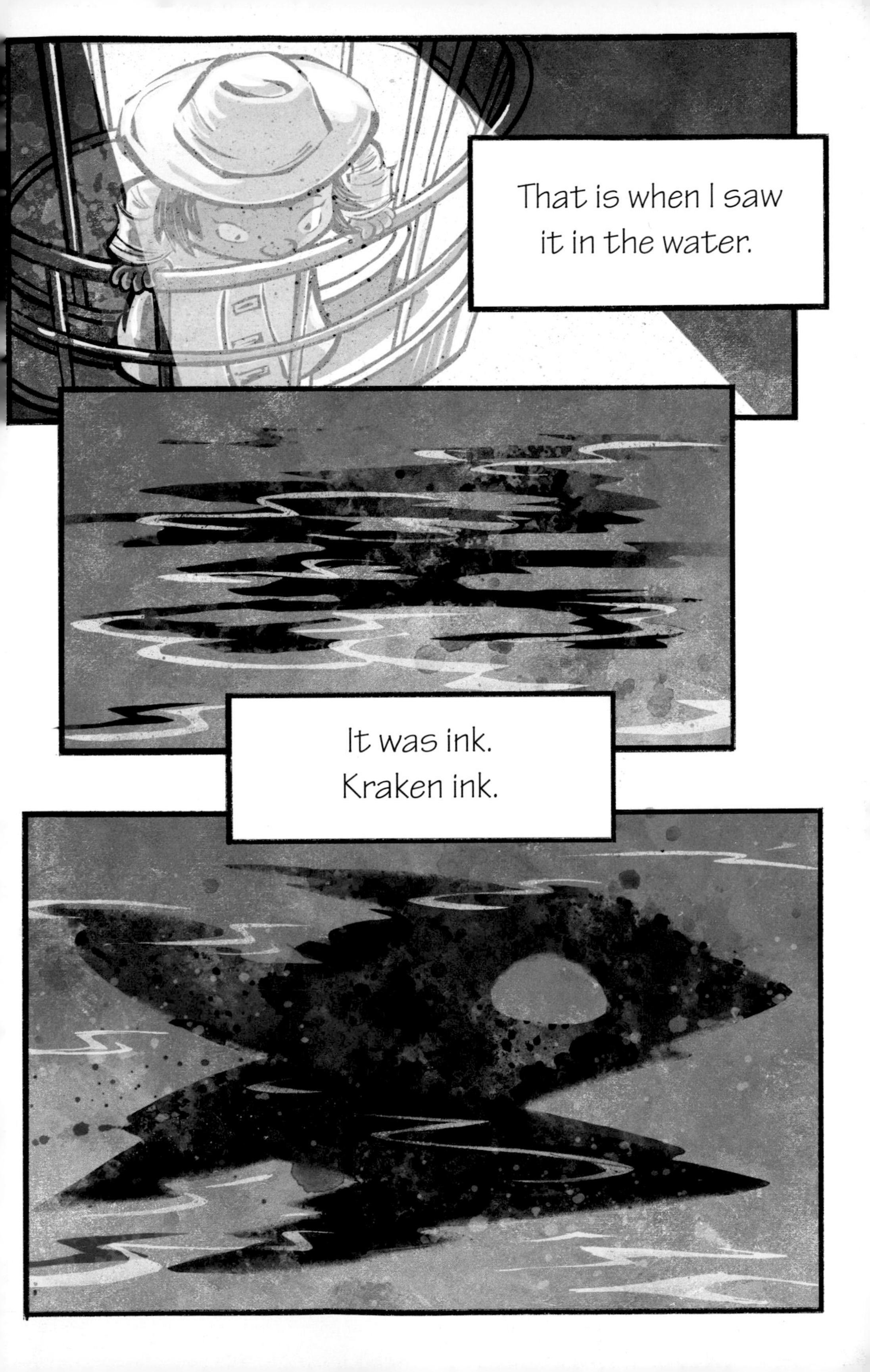
That is when I saw it in the water.
It was ink. Kraken ink.

At first he was scared.

Then he said hi.

A kraken cannot be in this show.
A kraken cannot be a pet.
Where is my kraken?
It is for the best.

Kraken?

I am sorry.
They do not know you yet.
They are scared of you.
Find a way to make them smile.
You can be in the show.

Let the show begin.
Our first pet is . . .

A KRAKEN!
No! Do not make him scared.
AAAAAA

AHH!

SPLAT!
If they are scared of you . . .

Yuck! Kraken ink.
. . . find a way to make them smile.
Dip

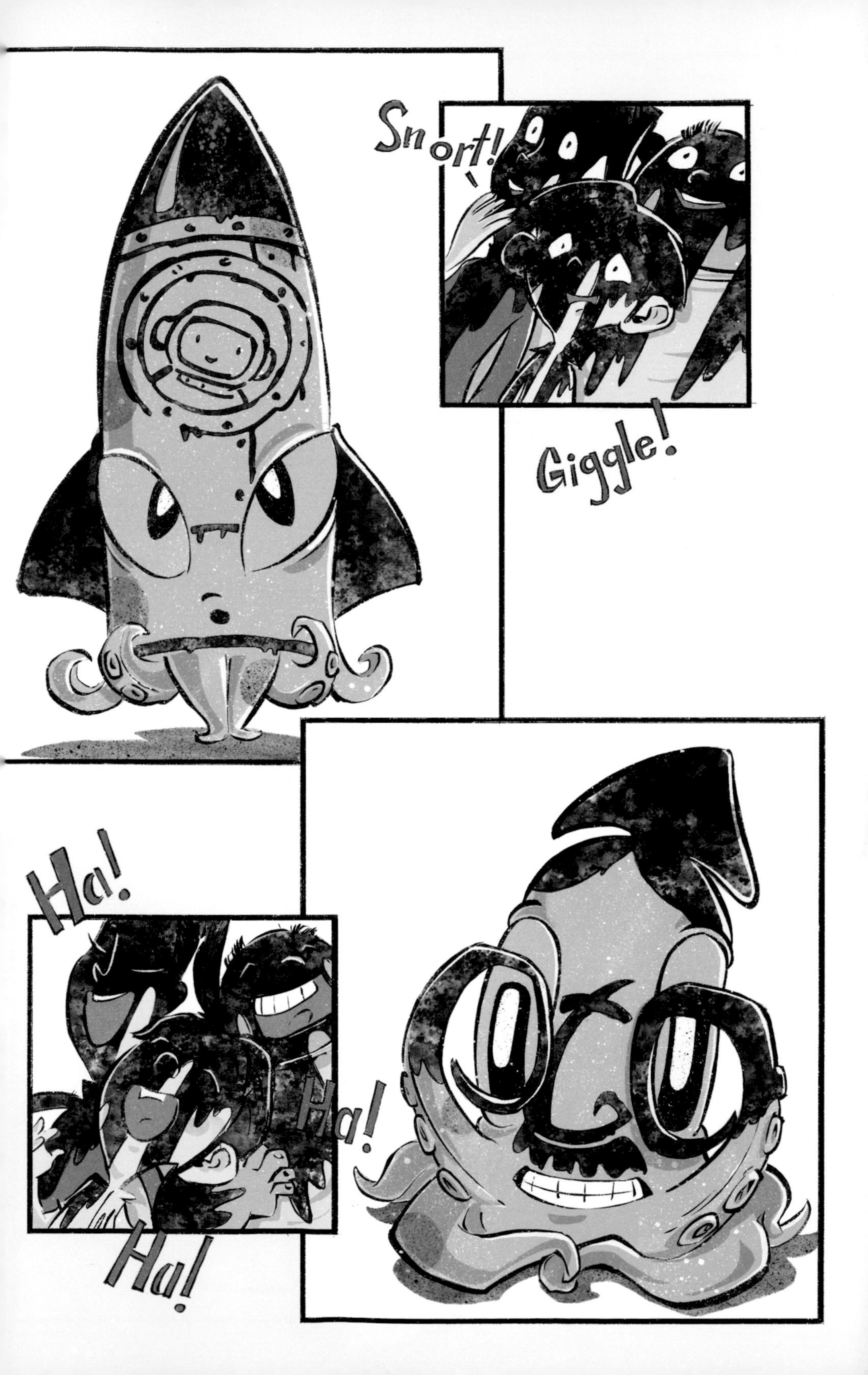
Snort!
Giggle!
Ha!
Ha!
Ha!

That kraken is crackin' me up.
I told you he was nice.

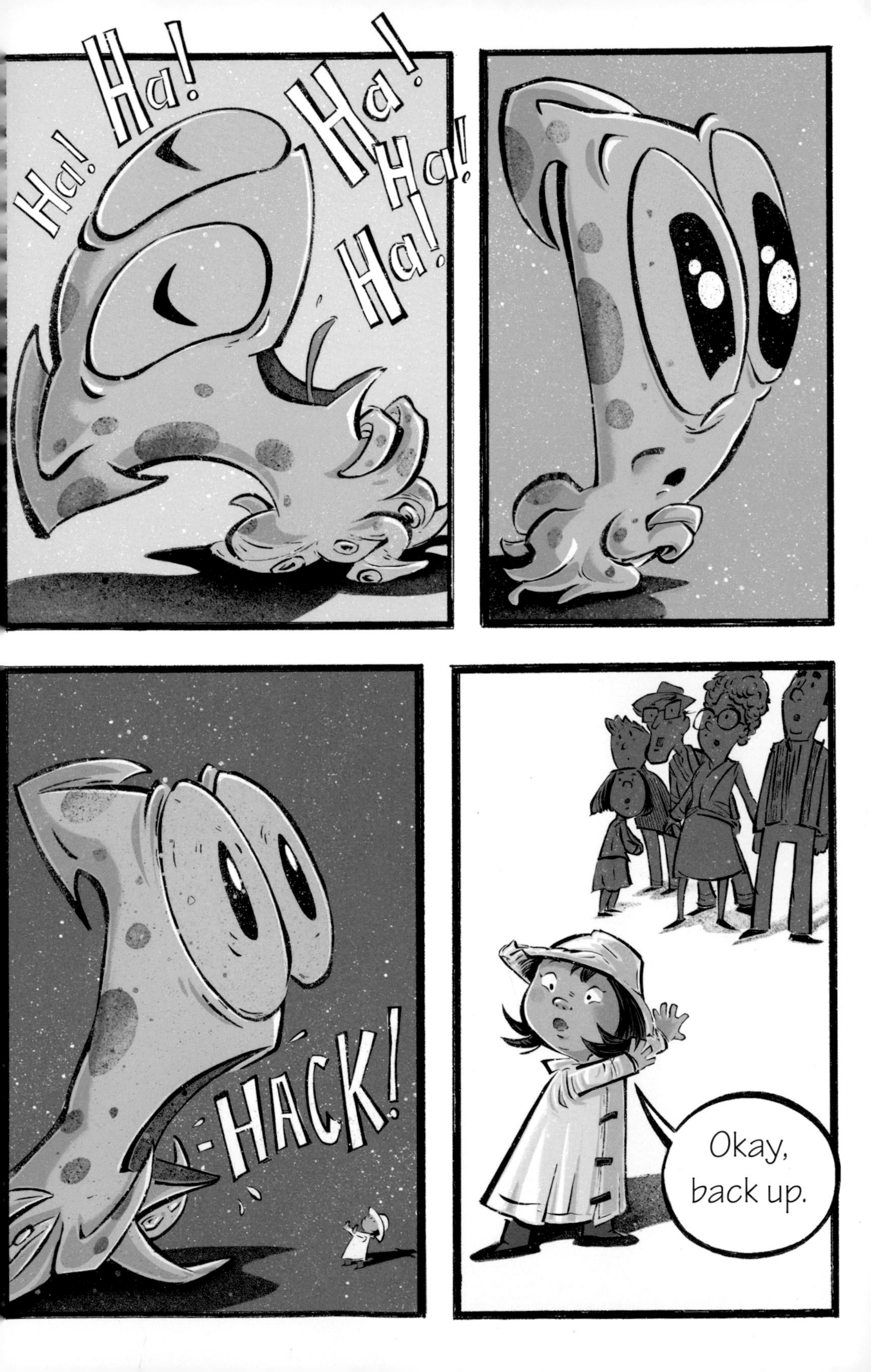
Ha!
Ha!
Ha!
Ha!
Ha!
-HACK!
Okay, back up.

That kraken
is hackin'!
HACK!

I told you they eat ships.

Hiccup!
Yar! We be in that belly for fifty years . . .

. . . so it's about time we had some fun!

NACHOS
EXIT

Fried Pickles
Fried Doughnuts
Refried Fries
Fried Shoes
Fried Salad
Fried Eggs

CORN DOGS

FOR MY DAUGHTER ISABEL,
WHO I'M SURE WOULD LOVE
TO HAVE A PET KRAKEN

I Like to Read® Comics instill confidence and the joy of reading in new readers. Created by award-winning artists as well as talented newcomers, these imaginative books support beginners' reading comprehension with extensive visual support.

We hope that all new readers will say, "I like to read comics!"

Visit our website for flash cards, activities, and more about the I Like to Read® series:
www.holidayhouse.com/ILiketoRead
#ILTR

Printed and bound in February 2022 at C&C Offset, Shenzhen, China.
The artwork was made digitally on an iPad with Procreate.
www.holidayhouse.com
3 5 7 9 10 8 6 4 2

Library of Congress Cataloging-in-Publication Data
Names: Ebbeler, Jeffrey, author, illustrator.
Title: Kraken me up / Jeff Ebbeler.
Description: First edition. | New York : Holiday House, [2021] | Series:
I like to read comics | Audience: Ages 4-8 | Audience: Grades 2-3
Summary: When Izzie brings her pet Kraken to the county fair everyone thinks he is frightening, but he is like Izzie, sweet and shy, and Kraken and Izzie use creativity and humor to win over the crowd.
Identifiers: LCCN 2021013010 | ISBN 9780823450176 (hardcover)
Subjects: LCSH: Graphic novels. | CYAC: Graphic novels. | Kraken—Fiction.
Pets—Fiction. | Humorous stories.
Classification: LCC PZ7.7.E25 Kr 2021 | DDC 741.5/973—dc23
LC record available at https://lccn.loc.gov/2021013010

ISBN: 978-0-8234-5017-6 (hardcover)
ISBN: 978-0-8234-5201-9 (paperback)

READ ALL OF THE I LIKE TO READ COMICS

Five Magic Rooms
by Laura Knetzger

Frog and Ball
by Kathy Caple

A Giant Mess
by Jeffrey Ebbeler

Spring Cakes
by Miranda Harmon